THE
POPCORN
TREE

BY CAROLYN MAMCHUR
ILLUSTRATED BY LAURIE McGAW

Stoddart Kids

Thanks to Gary Irvine, companion and colleague, for endless inspiration, and for sharing the childhood memory that sparked this story. Thanks to Kathryn Cole, editor and mentor, for her faith and wisdom and humor. Thanks to Eileen Mallory, secretary and friend, for her support and diligence. Thanks to my family. Boris, for the title. Mickey, for her genuine and infectious love of the spirit of Christmas. - C.M.

Thanks to Cody and Shannon Jamieson (Gary and Mickey), Paula Carlucci (Mrs. Tinsley), and Marg Smith (Aunt Rosa), who were my patient models. - L.M.

We acknowledge the Canada Council for the Arts and the Ontario Arts Council for their support of our publishing program.

Published in Canada in 1997 by Stoddart Kids,
a division of Stoddart Publishing Co. Limited
34 Lesmill Road
Toronto, Canada M3B 2T6
Tel (416) 445-3333 FAX (416) 445-5967
e-mail Customer.Service@ccmailgw.genpub.com

Published in the United States in 1998 by Stoddart Kids
85 River Rock Drive, Suite 202
Buffalo, New York 14207
Toll free 1-800-805-1083
e-mail gdsinc@genpub.com

Canadian Cataloguing in Publication Data

Mamchur, Carolyn Marie
The popcorn tree

ISBN 0-7737-2896-1

I. McGaw, Laurie.   II. Title.

PS8576.A5366P66 1997   jC813'.54   C96-930183-9
PZ7.M36Po 1997

Printed and bound in Hong Kong, China by
Book Art Inc., Toronto

PEEPS AND SIGHS

Downstairs, way downstairs, in one corner of a cellar, sat two raggedy-looking jumping jacks. They had been sitting there for a very long time.

Something else sat in a box in the cellar. Something small and very old. Something that made a sound. A sound like a sigh, a silver sigh, almost too silver to notice.

CHRISTMAS RAIN

Rain fell in big drops. Mickey and Gary pressed their noses against the window. They were hoping for snow.

Mrs. Tinsley reached into her cupboard and took out an old tin popper. She began to hum. The smell of popcorn filled the kitchen. The sound of popcorn filled the house.

Pop. Pop. Pop.

Next to the small box, sat a bigger box. From that bigger box came some even smaller sounds. Very small, too small for most to hear.

"Peep. Peep. Peep."

"Sigh."

"For the tree," said Mrs. Tinsley, pushing the big bowl towards her children. "And for you."

As they worked, Mrs. Tinsley told them about the olden days. "My mother's mother brought ornaments from England. Balls of blown glass, real candles. An angel with a dress of spun gold and wings of silver."

"I have to move," said Jumping Jack Boo. "I have to move soon."

"Then move," said his brother, Jumping Jack Lou.

"You know I can't move by myself."

"She'll never come down," said Lou.

"She never does any more," agreed Boo.

Their mother's words floated over the children like dreams. "I almost forgot the birds. Such small birds, fragile, all colors, with tinsel tails. And jumping jacks on strings, made by a gypsy, long, long ago. We called them Boo and Lou. Your grandfather would cut the tree and we would pull it home."

"To decorate on Christmas Eve?" asked Gary.

"With the glass birds and angel of silver and gold?" whispered Mickey.

"Yes, yes," remembered their mother. "I wonder if they could still be in the house where your Great Aunt Rosa lives?"

Two big tears rolled down the cheeks of Jumping Jack Boo, but his brother pretended not to notice.

Many tiny peeps came from somewhere nearby. And then there was nothing. Not a peep. Not a sigh.

The room was as still as old roses.

After Mrs. Tinsley had turned out the light, Gary and Mickey searched through their mother's desk.

They found old things, things as old as memory. And then they found what they were looking for. An address book with Great Aunt Rosa's name in it.

"We'll write to her tonight," said Gary.

"Yes, tonight," repeated Mickey.

"And then we'll have to wait."

On Tuesday, Aunt Rosa received a letter.

"Expecting something?" asked Mrs. Tinsley. "Expecting something in the mail?"

"No. Oh, no," said Gary.

"No, no, nothing at all," smiled his sister.

Aunt Rosa moved slowly. She hadn't been in the basement for a very long time. "Where are those old boxes?" she mumbled. "Where did I put them?"

Aunt Rosa always talked to herself when she was excited. "I'd almost forgotten those glass balls and the little birds. Oh yes, and the angel. Was there anything else?"

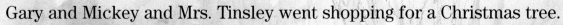

Gary and Mickey and Mrs. Tinsley went shopping for a Christmas tree.
"Should we decorate it when we get home?" asked Mrs. Tinsley.
"No!" answered Gary. "Not till Christmas Eve."
"If only we had the old decorations," said Mickey, her lips forming a small and secret smile.
"If only," sighed Mrs. Tinsley. "They must be long gone by now."
"Gone?" asked Mickey, the smile leaving her face.

The next day, Mrs. Tinsley got out their Christmas ornaments: wooden apples, thatched cottages, plastic snowmen looking as good as new. Looking as if they'd last forever.

The children watched. They didn't say a word.

Aunt Rosa mailed the package, still worrying that something had been forgotten.

When they heard her come back, Boo and Lou knew it was too late. The jumping jacks crumpled like a bag of bones. A noisy bag of bones, loud enough for Aunt Rosa to hear.

At last, two days before Christmas, Aunt Rosa's parcel arrived!
"What? What is it?" Mrs. Tinsley asked.

"It's our surprise from Great Aunt Rosa," beamed the children.

Mrs. Tinsley opened the old, grey boxes. She touched each bird. She touched each small and faded body. She touched each crushed and tarnished tail. Her hands trembled when she found the angel.

"Show us. Show us, Mother!" the children pleaded.

"Oh," said Mrs. Tinsley, her eyes so full of happy tears and memory, she didn't see how old and tired the angel looked.

But the children noticed. "She has no wings," Mickey whispered.

"Can we decorate now?" asked Mrs. Tinsley, her eyes all shiny with happiness.

"Okay," said Gary, his voice sadder and softer than he wanted it to sound.

"Sure," said Mickey, reaching for a plastic snowman.

"With those?" asked Mrs. Tinsley, her voice surprised.

The children saw the look on their mother's face. They dropped the plastic ornaments. "I guess we can use these," Gary said. He picked up a bird, old, tarnished, no good at all.

"We don't have to decorate now. Once, when I was little, we waited till Christmas morning," Mrs. Tinsley said, feeling something was wrong. She began, again, to tell her Christmas story. "Grandma always put on the angel. But Uncle Bert and I got to do the last, the best, the jumping jacks. We played with them. We moved them all over the tree. Boo and Lou."

"They didn't come," said Mickey.

"By tomorrow," promised the courier.
"For certain?" asked Aunt Rosa.

Night fell and another day passed. That evening the angel sighed, a tired sigh. Soft as a feather, too soft to hear.

Mrs. Tinsley sighed, a sad sigh.

The children sighed, a sorry sigh. Sorrier than no Christmas at all.

Only the birds refused to be sad. They poked their tiny beaks over the edge of the cardboard box. They could smell something. They could smell the popcorn. And they could hear someone. Something.

Gary and Mickey heard something, too. So did Mrs. Tinsley. Without a word they went into the living room.

One by one the small birds took flight.

"Oh, look!" Mickey cried, pointing to the door.
"What? Where?"
"Over there," Gary said, rushing to the door.
"The jumping jacks!" laughed Mrs. Tinsley.
"Boo and Lou!" the children shouted.
Mickey and Gary put Boo and Lou on last,
right where they belonged.

Outside it began to snow.
Inside everyone nibbled popcorn from the tree.

But the angel did not eat. She simply watched and smiled.
She wiggled her back. She had a small itch. She smiled again,
and wiggled some more. She knew what it was. New wings
were growing there. New silver wings.

The angel watched and wiggled and listened and smiled.
Then she sighed, a happy sigh. Soft as Christmas snow.